If We Should Ever Meet Again

RICHARD TREMBATH

First published by Busybird Publishing 2021

ISBN
978-1-922691-07-1 (paperback)
978-1-922691-08-8 (hardback)

Cover image: Richard Trembath
'Christine's Windmill'

Author photo: Kathleen Trembath

Cover design: Busybird Publishing

Layout and typesetting: Busybird Publishing

Busybird Publishing
2/118 Para Road
Montmorency, Victoria
Australia 3094
www.busybird.com.au

Also by Richard Trembath

More Lives Than One
(Pre-Press Concepts, 1996)

In the Company of Strangers
(Busybird Publishing, 2015)

Acknowledgements

Something I've learned is that books such as this don't just 'happen'. They are the result not only of the inspiration of the author but of the support network in the background, be they people who have provided that inspiration or those who have provided support, encouragement and, in some cases, the technical expertise required to transform some lines scribbled on a piece of paper in the middle of the night into a part of the whole. The fact that those lines have survived is, in part, a tribute to the many people I have to thank.

Most of those who have made some contribution know who they are, albeit that, sadly, some have passed on without ever knowing their true value in my life. Most notable among these is Sam Bickford, my English teacher at Geelong College, without whose initial inspiration none of this would ever have happened. Special mention must also be made of Nancy Helmore, Keith McGowan, Mavis Ellis and Christine Mogford, who played varied but integral parts in the transformation of those scribbled lines into something more.

There are many others who have believed in me and whose encouragement has been invaluable, most notable among them being Peter Byrne, Deverie De Ron, Deirdre Nedwell, Lyn Jamieson, Jennette O'Mahoney, Andrew Rule, Brian Tait, June Reeves, Sue Morris, Rosemary Henderson, Maureen Naylor, my son and daughter Jeffrey and Fiona Trembath, my grandson Cooper Trembath, and my publisher Blaise van Hecke, whose patience, guidance and professionalism has ultimately made the difference.

Contents

Poems

The View Beyond

Stories

Horse Tales

This Side of the Horizon

The Faces of Love

Days Before Yesterday

If We Should Ever Meet Again

Do you ever wonder
What would happen
If we should ever meet again?
Would it be like the first time,
Or the last?
They both seem so long ago,
And yet it is the first time I recall,
When we were in the springtime
Of our lives.

The days seemed longer then,
The road seemed straight and true
And yet life overtook us
With its twists and turns
And undergrowth along
The verges of the road,
More dense each mile
Until it blocked our long-shared view
Of life's true common goal.

You went your way and I went mine
Yet, looking back, I don't recall
The reason, what went wrong?
If anything. Perhaps it was just 'time'.
Time for both of us to scan life's landscape
As it lay, outstretched, before us.
We drifted, and our lives took
Different paths
To different destinations.

But what if, once again
Our paths should cross?
If we had time to pause, reflect
And to exchange the stories
Of our lives?
Would we change anything?
Or simply look upon those early days
With fondness, born of love,
And wonder why …?

The Gentle Rain

Rain ...
Gentle.
Where you are.
Where I am.
Connecting,
Walking rain.
Your soul, my soul.
Drifting, scudding,
Drawing us together
Across the waves:
Across space, across time,
To someday,
One day.
One day in ultimate time,
The day we walk together
In the gentle rain.

Beyond Dreams

I think I am beyond dreams – I have left it too
late;
In fact I'm not sure I ever had any – I was too
busy dealing with life
As it was.

So when do dreams drift from the future into the
past?
When do they go from anticipated plans
To unfulfilled regrets?
Is there a fork in the Road of Life,
Or merely a boundary – a line across the road?
And when is it we realise that plans or dreams
Involving physical endeavour
Are no longer possible?

Time is relentless – it does not wait for dreams;
Dreams take time to formulate
And even more time to fulfil
And if we dwell, we fall defeated
Along the edges of Time's road;
We find the dreams we let pass by
Are gone, beyond recall,
Transformed from dreams into regrets.

And yet, perhaps there *is* still time,
Perhaps the road is not yet barred
Perhaps there *is* another way, a side-road
Deviating from the road we thought
Was ours to tread
Inexorably beyond our hopes and dreams
Unto its end.
Another road? – perhaps.
Another dream?
Perhaps it has not ended yet.

We may yet find that other road;
And overcome the ravages of Time
And have our long-held dreams
Fulfilled, and find new dreams
And have our victory.
It is not over yet.

I Will Not Love You

I will not love you
In a way that will destroy me

But yet as something
Pleasant in my life,

I will not love you
Day by day or hour by hour

But oft' times dreams of you
Will haunt the night.

Though walls of stone
And gates of iron protect me

'Tis only you shall
Ever have the key,

So be my friend
And I shall not reject you

Enhance our lives
By being you and me.

Just a Falling Star

You flashed across my life
As does a star across the night
You blazed a trail, you left me stunned
And blinded by the light.

But all too soon 'twas dark again,
You went from whence you came,
And I my petty life resumed,
Before I knew your name.

And sometimes that's the way life is,
You glimpse it from afar
Your hopes you raise, then realise
It's just a falling star.

My Perfect Bride

Our souls will meet, my perfect bride
Within the depths of night
And magnetised become as one
And shine with lustre bright
Our bodies covet each to own
And glory in the night
And meet the dawn as one, enwound
Within our arms so tight.

The Colour of Your Soul

To write some lines as poets do
You said was surely not for you,
Convinced you had no tale to tell
You delved into an unknown well
And found there unimagined grace,
Confronted beauty face to face,
Your thoughts you found were flowing free,
Which came as no surprise to me.

The sparkling lines your pen produced
Revealed, excited and seduced,
Enhanced, as soft light from afar,
The tapestry of what you are,
Those few lines made the picture whole,
You showed the colour of your soul.

But Once

Softness, grace, and beauty,
    Peace,
Where have they gone?

Where are the days of yesterday,
The happy carefree days
    Of laughter,
    Hopes and joy,
The brief tranquillity
    Once almost captured
    Yet let slip, and lost
And ne'er revisited?

Yes, what is gone is truly gone
    And yesterday is over
    And its joy (if there was joy)
    Is just a memory.
We know within us
    oft' we say we shall return,
    'Next time', we say,
But next time never comes.

We get one chance alone
    And each one lost is gone
    And, ne'er can be regained,
But each one held, and
    Savoured, be it oh so brief
    Is beauty, truth, unblemished gold,
    A crystal moment of magnificence,
    Perfection,
And an insight
    Brief, provided into what
Makes this life so.

We must live now, while life is here
    And full and bursting forth to bloom,
For all too soon today
    Is yesterday
And love, and life
    The chance to live
    Has passed us by.

So grasp, and hold
    And live life now,
Not 'next time'
    For those words belong
    To cowards, they
    Who let
    Life's river flow on by
    And ne'er become a part of it
And hide from life, to get it
Over with.

But truth is here, somewhere
    Amidst the mire,
Peace, tranquillity,
    Beyond the throng,
    The noise, the cold
    Hard world that hems us in,
    Oppresses us where're we look.
Beauty comes,
    Not often,
But it comes.

But we too oft' ignore it
    And make not
    The most of these, our opportunities,
Our share of life's true nature

We avoid, side-step them
    Or, worse still, we fail
    To recognise them, so intent
    Are we
    On following the narrow paths
Of daily life.

To each shall come
    The vision, clarity of sight
    To recognise if only once,
The beauty, and the soaring heights
    Of Joy that this world holds,
    But when passed by, each moment wasted
    Goes,
And, having gone,
    Is lost beyond recall, unlived
    And shall not come again

And some lives pass
    Unlived,
    From dust, through flesh and life,
    To dust,
Unknowing what life holds
    Beyond their clouded field
    Of vision,
Never knowing beauty, truth or peace
And never knowing love.

He is no man, the man
    Who passes by this way
    With head held low, and
    Mind
    Ne'er asking 'What is this life
    All about?'
He breathes, he walks, he talks
    Yet leaves no mark of having
    Passed,
Or having lived at all.

I shall not go this way, for I
    Shall have but this
    One life,
And I shall, from this day,
    Seek all these things that go
    To make the essence
    Of this life
And I shall live
    Each moment for itself
    And life
    Shall not elude me.

The Seasons of Our Love

We missed each other's Springtime
because we were elsewhere.

Then Summer came, and left again
and still you were not there.

Soft Autumn, with its mellow tones
became our own lives' Spring.

We savoured it, and dreamed our dreams
of what each day would bring.

There seemed so many happy days
ahead for us to share,

We gave no thought to Winter
– but on a sudden it was there...

And all too soon we realised
the life we loved was gone,

The mists rolled in,
the dark clouds brought
 the cold and driving rain.

You left –

I can but shelter...
and hope we meet again.

Love Waits

Leaving …?
Once you are over the horizon,
It matters not.
Sight is sight,
Touch is touch.
Once I can no longer see you,
Or touch you,
Distance is irrelevant.
Love can stretch as far as
It needs to.
Love goes where you go,
Distance does not diminish it,
Love remains …
And waits.

On Parting

I cannot go and leave thee Love
    Denying all we had,
We must admit there was much good
    Before there came the bad.
When much is shared then much remains
    Regardless of what dies,
And there are things which can't be seen
By any other's eyes.

The bonds of love in early days
    Indelibly were writ,
'Though time corrodes and daily love
    Is stifled bit by bit,
There still remain those ties
    Which were by fears and hardship fused,
And they remain though all else die
And though love be abused.

If not as love they yet remain
    As mutual respect,
For fickle whims cannot destroy
    A bond with sweat stains flecked,
A bond which, made in happier days
    By two against the world,
Invited all to challenge it
To prove that it would hold.

Time changes all things and today
    Although our minds be clear
May prove in days to come to be
    Not as we see it here.
Perspective changes and our minds
    Depend on our surrounds;
They change, and thus our minds change
Within our vision's bounds.

Though new things come each day to change
    Our outlook on this life,
Few carry much significance
    And fewer cause us strife.
But some come as a sweeping tide
    Engulfs all in its path,
They are the tides of change and they
Bring with them aftermath.

And aftermath is what remains,
    What's left of you and I,
But though the flood has almost drowned
    It cannot make us die.
Though changes come to me and you,
    Though love's death see us part,
Time can't destroy what we have shared,
Nor erase you from my heart.

The Final Page

Write to me one day
And tell me of the second half:

Though we have gone our separate ways
To live our separate lives
I know enough of yours
To feel that I've read half the book,
And though it is no longer
Mine to read
I think of you occasionally
And wonder
What the unread chapters hold.

But even if I were to find the book
And learn somehow
Where life has taken you,
I know I'd never really know
The whole of it – your hidden mystery.

And I am well aware
That there would be
No point in skipping through
The unseen chapters, to find
Just how the story ends:

For it will end as we both
Knew it would – still unresolved.

The final page is missing.

Life, As We Live It

Without You

Without you this room is just a room,
    These walls are only walls.
Without you this day is just another day
    And I care not about it
And notice not if it be fine, or clear or dull,
    Or if it really be a day at all.
Without you I remain in limbo,
    Thinking not, nor doing, and without
Ambition
Save to see your face.

Without you I am just a shell, dormant
    And awaiting to be brought to life
By your mere presence,
    To be enraptured by your smile
Your touch, your spoken word.
    To feel the surge of life within my veins
Brought there by your existence and
    The knowledge unbelievable
That you are really mine
And that you care.

These walls become a haven
    And this room
The world,
    And I have no desire but to be
Alone with you; alone,
    Or in a crowd,
For just to be with you,
    Together, is alone.

To love you and to feel the bond
    Of warmth, intangible
But there,
    Invisible, and yet as real
As we ourselves.
    A bond of warmth and peace and confidence,
Serenity,
    Which though unseen
Could not be hid from any
Who observed us.

And I care not who knows,
    I want the world to know
And be a brighter, warmer place
    For having known our happiness.
And if it bring some joy to those
    Who walk this world without love,
Mere observers,
    That can but add more lustre
To the joy
    Of knowing that we have
What they have not and being
    Thankful
That it came to me and you.

Why we should be the chosen
    Ones I do not know:
All that I know is that we are
    And that we have each other
And that all else matters not.

Before you came the world was here
    And I was here
And I was in my way content,
Oblivious.

But now it seems unreal
    To think that in those days
Before you I imagined that I knew
    Of life.
My life began with you.
    My life revolves around you
And exists because of you.

Without you this room, is just a room,
    These walls are only walls;
This world is emptiness.
Without you.

Jigsaw

How testing is the task we face
To make the pieces fit
As we approach life's jigsaw,
Our own picture, bit by bit?

If we are blessed with fortune
And we quickly find a blend
Of matching colours close at hand
That make each tile a friend

They slowly start the picture
And with confidence it grows;
The more we build, the easier
To see where each piece goes.

But sometimes at Life's Table
There's a piece that's out of reach,
We know full well we need it
For our lives to be complete.

We know precisely where it fits,
The colours tell us so,
But if it's unattainable
We have to let it go.

And sadly it's too often so
In Life's imperfect mile
We can't complete the picture
For the lack of one small tile.

When Did the Roses Die?

Where did they go, the golden sands,
The beach I walked with you?
Where went the sun that shone
To grace the days when our love was new?
When came the tide, whence came the clouds,
The dark, the driving rain,
The cold that now engulfs the life
That I must live in vain?

When did the roses lose their blush,
The landscape lose its hue?
When did the sun that bathed our lives
Slip silently from view?
Where went the impish, joyful light
That twinkled in your eye?
Where went the love once brave and true?
When did the roses die?

Under the scythe of the Reaper Grim
And his vile whore, Neglect,
Who noiseless come in the night and cut
A swath when we least expect,
Who make us pay for each tiny sin
And each chance that we let pass by,
And leave us, amid the shreds of our lives,
To ask: 'When did the roses die?'

Where is the joy of the days lone gone
And the times I spent with you;
Of snow on the mountain and nights of rain
And strolls in the morning dew?
How did I lose you, where did you go,
When did life pass me by?
My memory still is of blood-red blooms,
When did the roses die?

Life's Path

You pluck'd me from woe's icy grip
And warmed my life again,
My soul repaired, my strength renew'd,
You dull'd my mortal-pain,
You made the storm clouds roll away,
You made the sky seem blue,
You calmed my shuddering, aching heart
And built my faith anew.

But life's paths do not always lead
Where we would like them to;
The path we plan and that we walk
We often find are two.
But moments cherished, moments shared,
Will last beyond the day
And though fate's twists encumber them
They will not fade away.

'Tis difficult sometimes to grasp
That all we have is now,
But well I know naught barr'd the way
Unto life's brink but thou.
These days we will remember, Love,
Not for their parting's pain,
But love, and truth, the joy we shared,
Which shall be ours again.

In the Company of Strangers

*We live our lives
in the company of strangers:*

How little we know of the hearts
    of the men who surround us;
How seldom we see but a glimpse
    of another man's soul.
We each tread our own destined journey
    that only we know of,
And strangers pass strangers, all bound
for the bell's final toll.

'Tis seldom we know of another man's
    thoughts or his essence,
Only *he* can decide what he shows us
    and wants us to see,
And if he decides to guard secrets and
    keep his own counsel,
He will never be known to the world,
nor to you, nor to me.

We're alone when we start on life's
    journey wherever it takes us,
And alone we will be, yet again,
    when we come to its end,
And in transit our lives are surrounded
    on all sides by strangers,
And the best we can hope for
is one we can truly call friend.

This Is Enough ...

What am I doing here, surrounded
By everything I've ever wanted,
Yet dissatisfied ...?

Why is it I still yearn
For something I have never known
And which probably
Is unattainable?

It makes no sense forsaking
The substance for the shadow,
Especially when the shadow
Is unknown, untested,
Just a fleeting wisp of fantasy.

The shadow holds no promises
But only hopes intangible,
Hopes that perhaps this time
The jigsaw pieces fit –
And comfort that they might.

So do I settle for the substance,
Still knowing that the shadow
Makes no promises, yet
Could deliver more …?

Do I allow my fantasy to strive
To seek a brighter, distant goal?

Just how far up the mountain
Do I climb before I pause,
Enchanted by the view,
And say: *'This* is *my* peak,
I climb no more. I am content,
I marvel in *this* view –
This is enough …'

On the Doorstep

You live your life in idle hope,
Without commitment,
Waiting always, anticipating that one day
The Universe will smile on you and send
Your long-awaited miracle
And make your life complete.

Patiently, you tread life's road, oblivious
But ever looking for a sign,
Unknowing that your gift
Has been there all the time
And that you've been stepping over it –
On the doorstep.

Corporate Irrelevance

We start our working lives believing
    we shall be rewarded
    by a grateful master:
But we learn that we are merely
    cannon-fodder – pay numbers
    in a computer run by people
    we do not know, who are themselves
    mere pay numbers in the same
    computer.
Our master is but a name
    – we know him not, he knows not us
    and when we go
    he knows not even we were there,
    much less that we are gone.

And Still You Wait

You wait at Gate Lounge B, the plane is late.
But then the board says 'Landed', so you wait.

The passengers emerge, at first a trickle,
Then great hordes of them, who all greet
Other friends – and still you wait.

Time passes and eventually you get to know
Your few compatriots, those who wait
For those who have not come – and still you wait.

Gradually patience turns into concern,
Your phone your only friend, but it is mute.
And still you wait.

The police stroll by and someone asks
'How many more inside …?'
'None' comes the stern reply, but still you wait,
Confused, concerned and unbelieving.

You send a text: 'Where are you …?'
Mind racing with imagined possibilities.

And then a message chime rings out –
It's yours, and gratitude floods
through your veins.

Relieved, you quickly read:

'Are you there already?
'I arrive tomorrow …'

But Not Forgotten

The magpie tree, towering beside the old dirt
road
Where the magpie used to swoop us,
Little kids, walking to school along the long
straight road
Across the Sandy Creek in days long gone.
The Sandy Creek, where the kingfisher had her
nest,
The pomegranate tree, beside the school,
Gone now, but not forgotten.
The little boys' collection of birds' eggs, well
recalled –
Blue ones, white ones, speckled, every size,
Nestling in their bed of cotton wool,
Missing only one – an eagle's egg …!
We tried, but an eagle is more than a match
For two little boys. All gone, but not forgotten.
And then the pony at full gallop down the street,
A little boy, riding bareback with a pussy willow
whip,
And the football match between two tiny towns
Separated only by the lazy river as it wandered
Through the verdant valley
Amidst the colours of the autumn trees.
All gone except the river, all long gone.
How sweet it was, the innocence
Of carefree childhood.
Long gone, but not forgotten.

Along the Way

Party Decoration

When do we cut the ribbons which connect us,
cease the pretence
of wishing to be the pillars of society,
respected,
looked upon as 'proper' by our peers
– 'the way we should be'?

When do we let go,
release our grip
on what we're taught are principles,
and they their grip on us?

Is it too late for our return
to basic instincts,
those which lie in wait
but shrouded
by 'the done and proper thing?' –

Man's pomp and babble –
cluttered now by overgrowth,
a tightly woven net
from which escape
becomes progressively less possible?

What holds us from our instincts –
lust, survival, will to live?
from blood and water,
warmth
and basic love?

When will we cease to care
what other people think
and live our lives not by indoctrination,
but rather
by what instinct taught us
as we left the womb?

And when will we discard
the 'window dressing',
that which makes us what we are
(or have become)
and robs us yet of what we truly are.

Courage, my friends,
and focus!
The world is so enamoured
of the illusion it creates
it can no longer recognise the truth
behind society's façade.
Ashes, dust,
flesh, blood and lust
– these alone are real.

The rest is fluff.
Inherited tradition.

Party decoration.

Time and the Road

Too short the time, too long the road
We should have travelled long ago.
But that was in another time
Before our paths crossed, yours and mine,
Both going on our separate ways
Pursuing dreams of other days.
Our journeys took us far away
But memories never left that day,
And now, our lives thrown far apart,
We, longing, share each other's heart
But anchored, each, by life's decrees
We cling to hopes as swift time flees,
And still we know each passing day
Sees love's fulfilment fade away,
Our hearts o'erburdened with life's load
Too short the time, too long the road.

On a hill beside the main Hobart Road, 20km south of Launceston, stands a lone tree. It was on this tree that, during the days when Tasmania was a penal colony in the early 1800s, the bodies of executed criminals were hung as a deterrent to passers-by.

The Tree on Gibbet Hill

BENEATH your dying, splintered boughs
   'Midst rocks the horses graze,
Your broken, withered limbs give not
   A hint of earlier days,
Days when you bore your dreadful fruit,
   When human life you craved,
When haunted, hell-bound sinners you
Denied the very grave.

The days when you defiant stood,
   A warning to the land,
Of Mankind's inhumanity
   And Death's swift icy hand;
The ghost of one such tortured soul
   They say lurks with you still
And curses those who scorn the dead
Who hung on Gibbet Hill.

But time is pass'd, men's ways are changed
   And your dread days are o'er,
You stand, a broken monument
   To times that are no more;
Perhaps when your time comes and you
   Return unto the earth,
Your passing will release the souls
And grant them second birth.

The highwayman, the murderer,
    The fool, the thief, the cheat,
Who rotted on your boughs denied
    The sinner's crimson sheet,
Denied in death the dignity
    Of but a pauper's hole,
Perhaps your death at last will grant
Repose unto his soul.

And you will be a legend, voiceless,
    Lingering in the night,
With no man left to tell your tale
    And naught to mark your site.
The land shall know tranquillity,
    The lost soul's voice be still,
As horses yet unborn graze 'midst
The rocks on Gibbet Hill.

The Bridge on The Road to the Gap of Dunloe

There's a bridge on the road
To the Gap of Dunloe
Where two streams meet and mingled flow
As one through Kerry's countryside
To join the River Loe.
We start our sacred journey
Where pilgrims trod before,
In view of Skellig Michael
On Ireland's western shore.
From the splendour of Killarney
We traverse this verdant land,
Its unmeasured miles of beaches
Deserted, untouched sand.
From the mystic, distant Skelligs
Our journey takes us still
To beyond the Kerry Mountains,
Conor Pass and Waterville.
To the holly trees converging
On the single-lane dirt road
And beyond the bend, a bridge
Inviting travellers: 'Rest your load'.
And beneath the bridge the merging
Of two sparkling, rippling streams
And ahead a horse-drawn wagon
Like a vision from a dream
As it plods on through the country,
All unhurried, slow,
Past lakes and rough stone fences
Heading north towards Dunloe.

Interpretation

The lines I write and what you read
Are not always the same
For what I mean is mine to know
My thoughts are mine to name.

Interpretation plays its part
Within the wider sphere
And what you read into my lines
My thoughts may not adhere.

You only hear the tale I tell
As it relates to you
You may not see within my words
What I and others do.

But your thoughts only add to mine
With an alternate view
And give the picture that I paint
A wider, deeper hue.

To not be easily understood
Is every poet's curse
But viewing through another's eyes
Enhances yet my verse.

The Day They Sold the Farm

Pigs, and grumpy cows
With shitty tails and leg-ropes,
Water-hens on the lagoon and eels,
Long, slithering eels that taste like castor oil.
Dog smells – waggy tails and licky tongues;
'Round 'em up, Spike, go away back ...'
And Marie, big clomping white furry feet
And big brown backside, way too wide.
'Can I have a ride, Uncle George?'
'Up you get, Son, hang onto her mane ...'
Milk cans and leather smells,
Wood-spoked milk-cart wheels.
'Can I drive her to the gate?
'Here, Son, hold the reins like this ...'
'Gee up, Marie ...'
And red-haired Rachel in the kitchen,
My God, where did he get her ...?
They don't make them like that anymore.
The Bakelite radio – who remembers Bakelite ...?
And *'Blue Hills'*, by Gwen Meredith –
'Episode two thousand four hundred and
eighty six ...'
Bessie, on the office wall. Butterfat ....
'She must have been a good cow, Uncle George,
To have her picture on the wall ...'
The old black Remington.
'Can I write something on the typewriter Uncle
George?'
Clackity-clack, grubby fingers,
Fix the ribbon, the keys are stuck again.

'At eight hundred and fifty thousand dollars ...
'Once ...!
'At eight hundred and fifty thousand dollars ...
'Twice ...!

Who cares how much?
You can't buy dreams
And little boy memories aren't for sale.

'At eight hundred and fifty thousand dollars,
For the third and last time and I sell ...

Done ...?
Done ...?
All done ...!'

Balloons

Nightdreams,
Daydreams
Black balloon
White balloon,
Drifting, seeking …
Seeking …
Floating across the miles,
Across the land,
Across the sea,
Across the world.
Narrowing the distance.
Out of sight
But drawn …
Ever closing
From the darkness to the light.
Magnetism, destiny.
Black balloon, white balloon,
Balloons of dreams
And love,
From your hand, my hand
To the winds –
To their predestined rendezvous,
To meet
And merge as one
In the twilight,
In the dawn,
Their trailing ribbons
Entangled
In their nakedness.

Darling

If she says, 'I answer to 'Darling','
That sure has to be a good sign
Especially if I can't remember her name
And she can't remember mine.

It happens when least you expect it
When the first word you think of is 'WOW'
And you know that you want to pursue her
But the obvious question is 'How?'

Then your eyes lock for one fleeting moment,
Just a moment, but frozen in time,
And you feel the world changing around you,
Then you glance back and look for a sign.

And you realise she's looking straight at you,
On her mouth just a hint of a smile,
So you think that it's now or it's never,
With your heart beating fast all the while.

As you take your first brave steps towards her
She comes to meet you halfway
And the world melts to mist all around you:
All your life you'll remember this day.

In the Middle of the Night

I wake into the twilight zone,
My dreams drifting, just beyond my reach.
'Go back to sleep', I tell myself,
Still clutching for my dreams --
They're gone.
What time is it? – Still dark.
A dog barks, just once, but it's enough.
Awareness now, a rush of wings, close –
The tree outside the window.
Moonlight flooding through the branches,
Across the floor.
The owl, I see it now… still… quiet
Silhouetted in the moonlight, waiting
For what…?
Beside me, body heat.
The soft moonlight caresses the warmth.
In the middle of the night, anything is possible.

The Hummingbird

I loved her,
But she was a hummingbird,
Flitting from tree to tree,
From flower to flower,
Seeking the nectar
Wherever she could find it.
Her tiny wings beat furiously
And incessantly.
She could fly backwards
If it suited her cause.
She left a trail of broken hearts,
But I loved her
And all I hoped was one day
She'd fly back to me.

You Are the Dawn

You are the gentle rain
And the moonlight that shimmers on still waters

You are the soft breeze
That lingers at the end of summer days.

You are the pink clouds' hues
Amid departing rays of sunset

And twilight on the far horizon
As it slowly fades to grey.

You are the endless stars, the diamond night
Before the first soft streaks of dawn

You are the dawn and all its promises,
The new tomorrow with its hopes of joy.

While Love Remains

We are never apart as long
    as I have memories of you
And you of me:

We are never apart as long
    as we can recall
The things we shared.

For as long as our memories
    endure and we care,
The bond will remain.

We shall never be apart for
    as long as memories shared
Are cherished by us both.

Though land and water
    may separate us,
They cannot separate our hearts,

For the Earth extends from
    where I am to where you are
And it is the same Earth:

I can touch it where I am and
    you where you are
And the Earth will link our touch.

I can look at the moon and
    know that you are looking
At the same moon:

I can drift through time and
    know it is the same time
I drift through with you.

We shall never be apart for
    as long as love remains:
We shall never be alone.

The View Beyond

Cartography

Have you ever made a road-map
Of your life
As it would be
The second time around?
Knowing, as you did, which forks to take,
Which to avoid.
Would it be different
To the one you've trod,
The one to which you're
Now committed,
The result of one wrong turn you made
So many years ago
When life was young?

You know you had your chance,
You can't believe you let it go,
It seems so clear now
In the cold grey light
As eventide draws near.

What would you change
If you could live your life
A second time
And with what consequence?
Where would you be?
What would surround you?
What would you miss
Of what you've created,
Which memories,
Which shining moments
In your tapestry of life?

What makes you think
You'd get it right
The second time around?
If you had the chance to
Go back to the start
With none of what you have
Or what you've done
Or who you've done it with
– No memory of it all –
Would you give it up,
The whole of it,
And start again?

Until There's None

It's hard to realise how much there was
Until there's none:
Conversation turned to silence.
Mere presence to aloneness.
Thoughts unshared.

To wake to greet the hollow day
And search for one good reason
To embrace it,
To become involved.
Not every day, but most.

To cast my mind back to
The happy times when you were here.
No need to speak, just simply 'be' –
Enraptured by each other's presence,
Our existence shared.

But now the all-pervading silence
Overwhelms me, robs me of the will
To go about my daily life,
To be aware of anything.
Nothing, save this stone that is my heart.

The Vision

From out the darkened realm you came
With light-bedazzled eyes,
A shooting star that briefly blazed
Across the midnight skies.

Your splendour turned the night to day,
The darkness into light,
But all too soon your blaze was gone
Unto the eternal night.

And all my mind is unsure now
If you were but a dream
And if my eyes alone saw what
No other's eyes have seen.

Morning Dew

(An epitaph)

Remember ye who walk there now
That once I walked there too,
And this same fate that's come to me
Will surely come to you.
Life's fleeting moment's quickly past,
Remembered by but few.
Remembered is the happiness
When life was fresh and new,
Remembered are the happy times
By those who shared them too.
They quickly pass, as pass our lives
Like sun on morning dew.

Tears Well ...

Tears well unto the eyes
Recalling yet
The happy times
Of long ago
Surrounded by the beauty
And simplicity
Of carefree youth;
Days in the sun
Without a care
Days when we still believed
The hazards of Life's road
Were not for us

But all that changed.
'Twas gradual at first
As childhood drifted quietly away
And we became a part
Of Life's eternal river,
With its rapids, and the banks
Withdrew beyond our reach
As yet the swollen torrent
Bore us, rushing now,
Upon its breast
Towards the endless sea.

How sweet the memories
Of all that came before;
Before we realised
Those golden days

Were just a prelude
To what was in store for us, our destiny,
Our predetermined journey
From the fields of joy
The days of childhood innocence
Unto Life's dark reality.

Tears well, from deep within;
We shed them silently, in rivulets.
Tears well
In thinking of those well-remembered days,
The days of long ago,
That are no more.

Our Winter Lives

They disappear more quickly in the
colder, barren climes
Where snow falls steadily and
covers them:
Two sets of footprints, yours and mine.

The snow blends, flake by drifting flake,
to cover them
And forms a pristine blanket, uncaring
where it falls and totally
Without discrimination.

Yesterday's snow, and all the indentations
which we made, together
In our lives, are gone,
with ne'er a trace that they were ever there.

The winding path – the one we trod –
is but a memory;
A fleeting recollection of a happy time,
but gone, to whence such memories go.

And now, that is its all – a memory –
and no-one cares *whose* memory, or why,
For that was yesterday.

But now it is another day, which brings
a new, fresh, pristine path, which all
Of us can choose to take; our chance to make
new footprints in the snow.

The choice is ours to write the text
of our new lives on Nature's
Clean white overlay, or, if we will,
withdraw, to dwell instead upon the loss
Of footprints made on other days; made
yesterday – and gone.

It matters not:

Too soon the sun – God's fiery orb –
will deem 'Enough!' It will be over.
And all the little secrets of our winter lives
will join the raging torrent as
It rushes headlong down the gorge
to join the summer sea.

Where We Live

There are two time states,
the past and the future,
which fit together perfectly.

Between them, in a place
which does not exist,
is the present.

This is where we live.

Lay Me Down

May my resting place be
At the foot of a tree;
A tall, strong tree
By the river's edge
Where the stream flows quiet
By the rocks and sedge.

Lay me down there
Near the south-east verge,
Which catches the rays
At the break of day
And the warmth of the sun
In its westward path
'Til the daylight wanes
And the shadows play
As the dark approaches
In fading light
And the bushland creatures
Withdraw from sight.

When all is quiet
Save the zephyr breeze
That lazily wafts
Through the riverbank trees,
The occasional sound of
Wings in the night
As a night-bird
Quietly takes to flight.

And I will lie resting
At peace with all,
As the world greets the rays
Of tomorrow's dawn.

The Melting of the Snow

My time draws near and I must go
Before the waning of the moon
Or melting of the snow,
Before all things that I hold dear
Are finally reduced to rubble.
While I am clear of eye and ear
And able yet to hear the
Chorus of the birds at dawn
And see the setting of the sun.
While yet my stride, tho' robbed of the bold
Fluency and strength of youth,
Does not betray me.
While all my being, slowed by time,
Has not yet reached the line which marks
The point of no return
Where all my will is lost
And dignity no longer marks the man.
While memory can yet retain the
Bold days of my youth
And the glories of the journey, which brought me
To this day which we all knew
Would come in time and now
Is but a few short steps away.
The journey has been hard but,
In its way, rewarding.
Of course I have regrets but sweet
Recall of days of joy and laughter,
Gone too soon but well remembered
Both by me and those I loved
Along the way.

There will be but few who mourn me for
Most of those whom I held dear have
gone before
But haply I will cross the thoughts
Of those remaining, briefly, from time to time
And I can only hope they will recall
A man, upstanding, in his prime,
Before the ravages of time
Brought him unto Life's final threshold
To which I now draw near.

And Time Will Pass

Time will pass,
   The wind will blow on by
And the water will flow over me
And I will be no more.

This day will come
   As surely as the setting
Of the sun;
   I will be gone
And soon I'll be forgotten.

Perhaps not straight away
   For those who knew me
May still, now and then,
   Have thoughts of me
But then, when their day comes,
   Those thoughts will perish
With them
And I will be forgotten.

For those who follow us
   Will not find time to care,
And even if, perchance,
   There comes one who will
Seek to know,
   He will but find my name—
Perhaps my work—
   And if it interest him
He then perhaps will dream
   Of days when I did walk this earth
And I could ask no more
   Than that, bemused, he wish
That he had known me.

For few of us will leave behind
    A mark of having passed,
Of having walked this land
    And having lived and loved,
Of having done the things that
    Make this life.
The sky will still endure on
    Through days when we are gone,
The land will still be here
    Though it be walked by other men
Who owe their lives to we who
    Walk it now;
But they will likely have too much
    To occupy their minds
To spare a thought for us,
    And if they do 'twill only be
A name they think about,
Which name is not the man.

No, I will be forgotten, and you too.
    And time will pass,
The wind will blow on by,
    The water will flow over us,
And we will be no more.

Horse Tales

The Horse Boy

He spent his Saturday afternoons sitting in the lounge-room listening to the Melbourne races on the big old radio.

He could get only one station, the ABC, but that was the one he wanted. Flemington, Caulfield or Moonee Valley – it didn't matter, if they were on, he'd listen.

There was a list of the fields in the newspaper, but it could hardly be called a form guide. Still, that didn't matter either – he knew all the horses' names, or the good ones anyway, and all the leading jockeys.

No-one was quite sure when his ritual started but later in life he was able to work it out, at least roughly. He knew he'd been born in 1942 and he remembered his two favourite horses, Red Fury and Fresh Boy, had run the minor placings in the 1947 Cup, won by Hiraji.

He was five that year but clearly remembered the Melbourne Cup. Jack Purtell, who rode Hiraji, was one of his favourite jockeys but he never really forgave him for beating Red Fury and Fresh Boy.

Later in the year, when he was in hospital with pneumonia, it was Red Fury and Fresh Boy he drew on the blank page of the puzzle book his Mum had brought him. Hiraji didn't get a mention.

That was his only memory of hospital but he must have been really ill because they'd rushed him there, the 70 miles from the tiny town where his father was the doctor. He was told, much later, he had had pneumonia, brought on by his coming home hot and sweaty from playing footy in the street with his mates and getting into a cold bath.

There weren't many mates because there weren't many kids in the town and the interest most of them had in common was collecting birds' eggs. Apart from finding them, he'd mastered the art of sticking a pin in each end, carefully blowing out the contents, then placing the shell in a bed of cotton wool in the box with the rest of them. The bigger kids were better at it than he was, but after a while his collection was the best in the valley.

That was a shared interest but none of the other kids was interested in the races. Most of them were interested in horses and a couple of the farm kids had ponies but he was the only one out of all of them who wanted to be a jockey.

It was all he'd ever wanted to be, as long as he could remember, which puzzled his Mum and Dad because no-one else in their families had ever had the slightest interest. Still, he'd been hooked since the day his Uncle George had put him on Marie, the old draught horse, and let him ride her as they took the milk cans down to the gate to be picked up and taken to the butter factory.

He'd never even seen a jockey, except for the pictures in the paper, but he knew they were little and he knew that in most races No 1 carried nine stone because it was the best horse. He couldn't read much at that stage but he'd heard the broadcaster say that Hiraji had carried 7st. 11lb, which was nearly a stone more than Red Fury and Fresh Boy. He didn't know what that meant – all he really knew was that the jockeys were small.

Anyway, the details didn't matter. What mattered was that there was a pony in a paddock at the end of the street and that he wanted to ride him.

The paddock was on the corner of River Road, which ran from the main street down to the river, about half a mile away. Why it was called River Road was a mystery to anyone who thought about it because it certainly wasn't a road – it was no more than a track which separated the paddocks on each side.

He knew the pony was friendly because whenever he went up to its paddock, it would come over to the gate and let him pat it. It was doubtful who enjoyed it more, the boy or the pony.

He considered himself an experienced rider because his Mum and Dad had taken him with them on a couple of occasions when they went to visit their friends, the Johnsons – Morrie and Johnno – on their farm 'out of town'.

The visit hadn't been for his benefit but he'd pestered Morrie to such an extent that he went and caught the old horse in the home paddock, saddled it up and gave him a ride. That happened on a couple of occasions and the second time Morrie had unclipped the lead and he'd been allowed to ride by himself.

The next time they visited the Johnsons he was told if he wanted a ride he'd have to go and catch the horse himself. No-one expected him to be able to, but he managed to manoeuvre the horse to the side of the yard then climb up the old wooden rails and clamber aboard. He had no control, of course, but when Morrie came out to check on him, he was happily riding around wherever the horse took him. His mother had been horrified but there was no harm done and the matter wasn't mentioned again.

In fact the only time that horses were mentioned was on Saturday afternoons when he settled himself down to listen to the races. At least that was the case until the day he decided to further his budding career as a jockey and went to visit the pony.

It wasn't as if it was far – after all, he and the other kids used to walk nearly two miles to school so walking up to River Road, past the pub and a few houses, was nothing. And there was no way his Mum was going to be worried about him – she'd just assume he was out playing with his mates, as he usually was when he wasn't at school. She knew he'd come home when he was hungry, or if it started to rain or get dark.

Sure enough, as soon as he got to the paddock, the pony came trotting over to the gate to see him. But today was different to other days.

He knew how to open the old wire gate and all he had to do was get the pony to stay still enough for him to be able to climb up the gate, grab a handful of mane and clamber onto its back.

It didn't ever cross his mind that anything could go wrong and as they headed out onto the gravel of the main street, all he could think of was that he was his very favourite jockey, Scobie Breasley, bringing Red Fury up behind the barrier.

Then they were racing. He crouched over the pony's neck, hanging on tightly to two handfuls of mane as they gradually built up speed and charged down the street, past the houses, past the pub and past ...

He'd heard the crowds at the races cheering on the radio but this time there was only one voice and it was calling his name.

The doctor's surgery, where he lived, was only a couple of houses past the pub and had a small, neat garden which welcomed the patients as they came through the front gate.

And working in that small, neat garden was his mother.

He didn't know, but she had looked up as she heard the galloping hooves passing the pub. Her reaction accounted for the 'cheering crowd' noise as the pony and his rider hurtled past the surgery, heading for the far end of town.

The boy and the pony were far too excited to recognise the voice, or realise what it meant. But the pony wasn't used to vigorous exercise and by the time they got past the post office and general store, he was rapidly running out of condition.

The boy was elated but the pony was heaving and blowing as the boy turned him around and headed back, walking slowly up the street towards his paddock. It was then that the boy realised where the cheering crowd noise had come from.

He had never seen his mother run, but here she was, heading towards them, screaming at him. Sure, she'd reprimanded him on occasions in the past, but he'd never seen her cry and she certainly had never yelled at him before. His excitement dissipated quickly, at least on the surface.

He knew better than to say so but, despite how upset his mother had been, what happened that day and the sense of achievement it gave him were among his most cherished memories for the rest of his life.

His parents were hoping the boy's interest in racing was just a passing phase, but he never wavered, either in his interest or in his ambition to become a jockey. At least he didn't until one day several years later.

His mother had a ritual – every year on their birthdays, she would mark his and his sister's heights on the wall, with their weights beside them. He had never taken much notice until his tenth birthday when he saw what she had written beside his height – 7.00.

Seven stone …!!

Exactly the weight Red Fury had carried in the Melbourne Cup.

Suddenly he realised what that meant. Half the Cup field had carried lighter weights than that, and those jockeys were grown men …!!

The dream was gone.

He had to stop growing but how was that going to happen when he was only ten? He tried to stop eating, but that was never going to last for long. He was ten years old and already he was too big.

His life and his ambitions took a different direction, but he never lost his love for the horses or the jockeys or the thrill of the race. Later in life he would go to the races and absorb the atmosphere – to marvel at the sheen on the horses' coats, their haughty pride, the kaleidoscope of colours of the jockeys' silks as they sparkled in the mounting yard or came charging around the bend. The sounds and smells of the racecourse. But he was on the wrong side of the fence.

He often thought about the pony and just as often he'd catch himself looking at the jockeys behind the barrier stalls, whether it was at Flemington, or Royal Ascot, or Kalgoorlie, or Birdsville.

It made no difference whether he was at the races or watching on TV, the thought was always the same:
  'Have you blokes got any idea what you've got?
  'You've got what I've wanted all my life.
  'You're living my dream...'

No Big Deal

There was a time when I thought it was a big deal to get your name in the newspaper.

It had started the Saturday morning I met Brian in the showers at the boarding house. We weren't exactly 'in' the shower together, but we were in the bathroom, which was pretty basic – several shower heads but no cubicles nor concession to modesty.

The eighty-odd occupants of the men's boarding house came in all shapes and sizes and you never knew who you might meet in the bathroom. Anyone with any pretentions to shyness or modesty quickly found that either you ditched those or you ended up waiting for quite a long time if you wanted the bathroom to yourself. And even then, you never knew who might walk in.

In any case, Brian and I quickly established that our plans for the day were identical – we were going to the races at Moonee Valley. That, of course, led to the obvious discussion about trying to back a winner. And after a while we came up with a plan.

It was 1960, in the days of pounds, before the introduction of dollars. Neither of us had much money and having a pound on a horse was a pretty big bet for either of us. But this day we had both courage and confidence in our ability to beat the bookies.

We'd studied the form guides and agreed that in the first race, there were only two horses who could possibly win – New Statesman and Cotillion. They were equal favourites, both at 2-1. Obviously an outlay of a pound on each of them was going to result in collecting three pounds – a profit of a pound. It was watertight – none of their opponents was any good, so we set off for the races to execute our plan.

Now in most stories about racing and betting, something goes wrong, but not this day. New Statesman and Cotillion were both 2-1 and they fought out the finish. Which one won was irrelevant – we'd each come to the races with two pounds and now we had three. We were geniuses but more importantly we had formed a friendship which would last for life.

That friendship resulted in another 'shower connection', which played a part in me getting my first job as a journalist, at the Wimmera Mail-Times in Horsham, a year or so later. Not having a car and with very limited resources, I hitch-hiked to Horsham for my interview.

It was a hot summer's day and by the time I got to Horsham I was in no state to make a favourable impression at an interview. Luckily, however, Brian had a cousin in Horsham and had arranged for me to go to his place, have a shower and change into some respectable clothes.

Again the plan worked – I got the job. Even better, as it turned out, the sports writer at the paper didn't like the races or the trots. After a few weeks ascertaining whether or not I could actually write, the editor asked me if I'd like to be the racing writer.

How good was that …? Not only did I get to go to the races and the trots every Saturday but I got paid for going …!! And my tips in the paper …!! – a column next to the race fields headed 'Richard Trembath selects'. Life was good – I was 19 and getting my name in the paper in bold type.

Every Saturday I went to the races at the bush tracks around the Wimmera and one day I found myself at Nhill, which boasted about the same standard of facilities as the rest of them.

There was a bar, of course, but no toilet block, only a country 'dunny' halfway up the hill behind the betting ring. There was nothing 'upmarket' about that either and certainly no nice soft toilet paper – just torn up sheets of newspaper on a rusty nail, in keeping with most country sporting venues in those days.

Anyway, at one stage of the afternoon, I found the need to 'go'. Ultimately, sitting there thinking about nothing in particular, I reached for the first sheet. And there it was: 'Richard Trembath selects' in nice bold print.

I carefully folded it and put it in my pocket.

Not since then have I ever thought it was a big deal to have my name in the newspaper.

Never Lay Odds-On

Back in the days before technology flooded the racing industry and other sports flooded the newspapers, it was the usual thing for the racing staff cadets from the metropolitan dailies to attend and cover the Saturday country races.

In those days there would be meetings at such places as Woodend, Ballan, Heathcote, Hanging Rock, Burrumbeet and quite a few others.

Usually these tracks didn't have 'betting supervisors' and part of the cadets' task was to provide the official statistics of the meeting – the starting prices and finishing order in each race – to the club secretary, who would pass them on to the appropriate authorities.

The cadet would collect an additional racebook (and a lunch ticket, of course) on his arrival and for the rest of the afternoon, whatever he wrote in that second racebook was 'official'.

Now, without saying this ever happened, it does not take a lot of imagination to work out that if the cadet was a punter, he could manipulate the details in his favour and create a situation in which he couldn't lose and his favourite SP bookie couldn't win.

Starting price bookies flourished in those days and there's not much doubt there was more money bet with them than with the on-course bookmakers, who could number a couple of dozen, maybe more.

One of the cadets' responsibilities was the 'run-on', the finishing order in each race, and occasionally a spectacular and unlucky effort by, say, the sixth placegetter, might be 'missed' and the horse placed second-last in the official results.

Of course that could lead to that horse being at an inflated price the next time it stepped out – after all, there were no videos and a last start 13th at Woodend wouldn't read quite as well as a last start sixth. But let's just concentrate on the business of 'making a quid' on the day.

These were the days before mobile phones, of course, and apart from the phone in the secretary's office, the only other one on the course was in the Press Room. Mostly it was used to ring through results to a copy-taker at the afternoon paper and there was never any record of who made the calls, or who they rang. So it was quite possible that not all the calls were to the copy-taker.

Just for the sake of simplicity in telling our story, let's say the principal characters were Tom, Dick and Harry.

Tom and Dick were cadets on the staff of one of the metropolitan dailies while Harry was an SP bookmaker who was not afraid to take a bet, as evidenced by his laying one punter $14,000 to $7000 about General Command when he won the Sydney Cup of 1968.

Tom and Dick were established customers but seldom had a substantial bet, unlike some of their workmates. The other rule they stuck by was that they *never* laid odds-on.

And this was their key to success.

Harry was aware of this and thought nothing of it when one of them had a bet on a short-priced runner with the stipulation that if it started odds-on, there was no bet.

Having set this in place, Tom and Dick had a regular Saturday routine. One of them would go to the country meeting while the other sat at home, next to the phone.

Occasionally the phone would ring and the voice on the other end would say: 'We've got one – number seven, Royal Dress'.

Tom, sitting at home, didn't need to ask what race or where, he already knew all that. All he had to do was hang up and dial Harry's number.

'It's Tom, Harry, Woodend race six number seven Royal Dress, $400, odds-on, no bet.'

Harry would confirm the bet and, for the boys, it was 'game on'.

Tom and Harry knew that if Royal Dress won, the bet would be settled, in cash, the following Tuesday afternoon at the pub over the road from Tom's office.

Tom might have a couple of other bets of, say $30 or $40, during the afternoon. If they won, they won, if they didn't, it didn't matter too much – their main purpose was to deflect any thoughts Harry might have about the boys' big bets winning with monotonous regularity. By Harry's standards, they weren't big bets anyway and Tom and Dick were careful to keep it that way.

And they were also careful that their main bets were only on horses who were about even money in on-course betting. That way no-one was too surprised if, having been beaten, the favourite's price was returned at odds-on, say 9-10, or if, having won, it had drifted in the last minute or so of betting from the evens most of the bookies were betting to, say, 5-4.

To Harry, the fact that either Tom or Dick lined up to collect three or four hundred dollars on a Tuesday afternoon was no big deal – it didn't happen every week and he had 'bigger fish to fry'.

But it was a handy supplement to the incomes of a couple of kids who in those days earned about $80 a week.

During his journalistic career, the author founded what originally was Victorian Trotting Weekly, later to become Australian Harness Racing Weekly, and was editor for more than 20 years. The following story was published in June 1989 and won the Australian Harness Racing Council's 'Joseph Coulter Award' for the year's best story in all categories of its awards. It is a true story.

Rest Easy, Girl…

One evening last week, an old mare named Moonlight Sky lay down for the last time and peacefully drifted off to horse heaven.

'So what?' you may ask, and with some justification, for nowhere is her name chipped in stone, nor is it to be found among the list of Australian harness racing's all-time greats.

Only if you can remember trotting as it was in Western Victoria in the early 1960s, or if you are an ardent student of breeding would you be likely to have heard of her.

But if there had been no Moonlight Sky, I greatly doubt there ever would have been a 'Trotting Weekly', or certainly not one as we know it today.

I first met 'Helen', as I always knew her, at the Wright Stephensons' sales complex, over the road from Flemington Racecourse, on July 1, 1963.

At that stage I had been working as a cadet journalist on the Wimmera Mail-Times at Horsham for about 18 months, spending most of my days off at the stables of the Wimmera's most prominent trainer, Jack McKay, at Minyip.

My 'landlord' and friend, Max Parish, who was the top driver around the Wimmera circuit at the time, worked for 'Minyip Jack' and gradually taught me the basics of the trotting business.

Learning to drive was a slower process because, initially anyway, the lessons had to be conducted when Jack wasn't looking, which usually meant waiting for a day when he was away inspecting his sheep or on some similar mission.

In any case, by the time I'd been at Horsham a little more than a year I'd decided that if I was going to be mucking out stables and working a horse, I might as well be doing one of my own.

I well recall that at the time I was earning three pounds seven and six a week (the equivalent today of $6.75) and I reckoned I could afford maybe 20 or 25 pounds to get a horse.

Even then you couldn't get much for that sort of money, so I arranged with a friend (who knew considerably more about horses than I did) to 'go halves'.

We decided to go to the Wright Stephensons' winter mixed sale but unfortunately a few days beforehand he was injured in a horse-related accident and finished up in hospital.

So I went to the sale by myself.

As anyone who knew 'Minyip Jack' McKay would know, it would be impossible to be around him for long without absorbing at least a basic knowledge of Standardbred breeding, so I was all right on that score and recognised from a look in the catalogue that the unbroken two-year-old filly by Noble Scott from the Silver Peak mare Romantic Silver, a grand-daughter of Walla Walla, was pretty well bred.

So I went and had a look at her.

She certainly was no 'oil painting' but she had four legs, one on each corner, and there didn't seem to be anything wrong with them, or with anything else so far as my untrained eye could spot immediately.

In retrospect I realise that had I not been quite so impatient I might have got her for less than 40 guineas ($84) as my bid turned out to be the only one.

Nevertheless, suddenly I was the owner of a horse (or part-owner anyway), so I hitch-hiked back to Horsham quite proud of myself and a couple of days later went and collected her from her own personal cattle truck at the railway station and walked her through the back streets of the town to her new home, in a stable at the Showgrounds.

It was a few days before my friend was discharged from hospital and by that time Helen had been wormed, cleaned and fed to the extent that her appearance had improved considerably.

He took one look at her and almost had a heart attack.

"You don't expect me to give you 20 guineas for that, do you?" he exclaimed.

Suddenly I was the sole owner of a horse, but I was also short of 20 guineas I had been depending on to buy some gear.

To make a long story short (or shorter, anyway), veteran Horsham horseman Les Jones came to my rescue, loaning me a set of harness and hopples and a few months later Helen was ready to race.

Her first start was at her home track and I will remember it as long as I live.

It was not only her first race but also my first race drive and I didn't have the slightest idea how either of us was likely to react once we got out there under the lights.

But even getting there seemed for a while that it might be a problem.

Helen – whose racing name for the first few starts of her career was Helen Of Troy – put on an act in the mounting yard, breaking a hopple carrier, which was hastily repaired with a piece of hay band.

Not being too sure about anything, I invested not a solitary shilling on her, so it came as something of a surprise that, when I pulled her out from midfield in the back-straight the last time, she suddenly grabbed the bit and began to swoop on the leading group of four, who had got away in front.

In the circumstances it seemed unwise to go three-wide around the last turn, so we headed back for the rails and eventually went to the line in a pocket, finishing fifth to

Sampson Direct, who later turned out to be a pretty handy horse.

At her next start, around the two and a half furlong 'saucer' at Ararat, Helen drew the second row in a field of 14, got flattened at the start and was never in the race, finishing second-last to Baroda's Return.

With the two races 'under her belt' Helen was starting to learn what it was all about and her work started to indicate that she had enough ability to win a race.

But I was determined that if she did, it was I who was going to get the benefit and not all the 'smarties' who hung around the Horsham Showgrounds, and who had virtually queued up with my former partner to ridicule the bag of bones I had brought home from the sale.

So I let them think I was giving her an easy time, only ever letting them see her doing light jog work.

In the meantime, however, I was getting up early on 'fast mornings', riding Max's wife's bike to the track and working Helen while it was still dark.

She got to the stage that I thought she was going pretty well, then one day I got Max to come and have a drive on her to see if I was on the right track or merely going mad.

We worked her 'outside the hurdles' (which were put up to protect the inside of the track) in the middle of the afternoon when there was no-one around.

I can't remember exactly what time she worked, but I do recall that it equalled the track record, which at that time was held by top-line free-for-all performer Rising Flood.

Max and I were beginning to get hopeful, but we had to be sure.

So we took Minyip Jack into our confidence and the following week, watched only by the crows, we trialled three horses together at the Sheep Hills racecourse.

Jack drove Newport Dream, who at that time was a metropolitan class free-for-all horse, Max drove the rising star of Jack's stable, a filly named Skirl, and I drove Helen.

Newport Dream beat Helen by about a neck, with Skirl back in the dust. We had a winner – all we had to do was get a run somewhere and draw a decent barrier.

Our chance came on Boxing Day, 1963. Helen drew No 3 in a field of 15 with a ready-made favourite in Cita Sea, a smart filly who was later the dam of an even smarter one, Cita Dollar.

It was then that I did one of the few really smart things I've done in my life.

Despite the fact that I loved driving and would have 'killed' to have driven a winner, I swallowed my pride and decided that as Max knew more about driving than I did and I knew more about punting than he did, we'd better do it that way.

Jack agreed to the plan and scratched his two runners to leave Max free to drive Helen and me free to organise the betting.

I rounded up all the money I had in the world, which amounted at that time to 52 pounds, 'conned' a lift to Charlton for myself and my horse, and set off in quest of fame and fortune, or fortune anyway.

The short version of what happened is that we backed Helen from 33-1 to 6-4 and she did the rest, jumping straight to the front and leading throughout for an easy win.

It had cost me a pound to 'pay up', I had kept a pound to start my life again if anything went wrong, and had the rest on Helen.

I was earning about 170 pounds a year at the time. My winnings, 612 pounds, represented about three and a half years' pay.

Later in the afternoon a prominent owner came and offered me 800 pounds for my filly.

I was certainly younger and possibly sillier in those days, but I well remember my reply.

"Mate," I said, "I've got more money than I knew there was in the world – what would I do with another 800 pounds?"

At times we all have occasion to think of what one event has provided the highlight of our lives. There has never been much doubt about mine.

Helen went on to record four wins and 18 placings from about 40 starts before suffering horrific injuries in a training fall at the old Ballarat track one morning when she was a five-year-old.

There had been a football match there the day before and Max, who had moved to Ballarat and was training her at the time, had gone around beforehand with his workmate, clearing the leftover cans off the track.

Unfortunately they had missed one; Helen jumped it and came down 'like a ton of bricks'.

Her injuries, without going into them in gory detail, were such that the vet wanted to put her down.

But Max and his wife, Bev, insisted on at least trying to save her.

For several weeks Helen's life teetered ominously close to death's door but gradually it became apparent that all the work, the nursing and the care were going to pay off.

Eventually she came home to Yarrambat, where I was living at the time, and finally the last dressing came off exactly a year from the date of her fall.

Helen carried the grim reminders of her accident for the rest of her life but she nevertheless was able to go to stud, producing two winners, Skylarkin and Top Flat, both by Aachen.

Top Flat won numerous races, including three at Harold Park in Sydney and several in the US, while their sister, Aix La Chapelle, went to stud without racing and produced handy performer Aix La Charisse and Tipperary Sky, the dam of former top juvenile Tipawin.

Not much of that is relevant, though, because I promised Helen that day at Charlton that she had a home for life, and whether or not she had foals was never going to make any difference to that.

I am well aware that some of the more cynical of my colleagues – and perhaps our readers, too – will brand this story what one I can think of so graphically describes as "self-indulgent wank", but I couldn't give a damn.

I know that for everyone who thinks that, there will be dozens who at some stage of their lives have had a 'special' horse, whom they loved, and who will be able to identify with this story.

Helen was not a champion, but we came a long way together and I have little doubt that but for her I would have drifted out of harness racing and would not be where I am today.

She was a lovely horse, who changed my life.

I have no doubt that of all the people who have ever had the experience of knowing and loving a horse, most have a tale they could tell.

This has been mine.

This Side of the Horizon

Writer's Block

It came as a shock to realise that, having spent most of his life earning a living from writing, he had no imagination, or hardly any, anyway.

Sure, he could write, he knew that, but gradually it dawned on him that mostly what he wrote was about events, happenings – things that existed or which, in one way or another, he'd observed.

He had wondered for a long time, maybe years now, why his head had been creatively empty. He'd been reasonably prolific at one stage, but hadn't written anything worthwhile in ages – almost as long as he could remember.

There'd been the poem he wrote after Christine died, of course, but that was different. He knew it was good, or at least he thought it was, but it was born of emotion. It hadn't just come from nowhere – it had taken an event to prick his creativity. And it wasn't just 'creativity' – it was emotion, spilling onto the page. Even now he couldn't read it without his eyes welling up.

One well-meaning admirer of his work had suggested at one stage that he read it at one of the poetry-reading nights he attended from time to time. Read it…! He doubted he'd even be able to look at the page in front of an audience without 'losing it'.

He wanted to write, he knew that, and the myriad journalistic awards and a couple of published books testified that he could, but he also knew you can't write about nothing. He imagined his skull, vacant. He'd heard of 'writer's block' but how long could that last? Forever?

Sometimes he compared himself to John Keats, not in talent but in representing the opposite ends of the spectrum of productivity. One of the Keats quotes he knew was:

*'When I have fears that I may cease to be
Before my pen has gleaned my teeming brain…'*

Teeming brain! Where do you get one of those? He knew Keats had one because, after all, he had died at age 25 but is recognised as one of the great poets of the English language.

But how do you become as prolific as Keats, he wondered? Keats, who apparently had the ability to create masterpieces 'out of the air'.

Simple – imagination…!

At least a fertile imagination can produce quantity, albeit that quality requires talent.

He'd heard that the best way to defeat writer's block was to simply sit in front of the keyboard and start writing. Of course Keats didn't have a keyboard, but in his day that probably equated to picking up a quill.

One of the facets of writing fiction he had always enjoyed was the *power* – the ability to be God; to make your characters do what *you* wanted them to do. The knowledge that, if you got tired of a character, or he somehow offended you, you could throw him under a bus.

That wasn't recommended, of course, in the middle of a 'semi-serious' story totally unrelated to buses, but the fact remained – if it took your fancy, you could do it.

But where was this story about the lack of a story actually going? Well, nowhere really. Back around the block, to where it started.

And we all know which block that is, don't we….?

Starting with 'F'

How is it that Jill Fanvula wandered through my dreams? I'd never heard of her, in fact I'd never heard the name 'Fanvula', if such a name exists. And as far as I remember I've only known a couple of Jills in my life, one with whom I worked forty years ago and haven't seen since, and one who is long dead.

Yet there she was – Jill Fanvula, as large as life, or at least as close as you can get to that state in a dream.

She was attractive – mature, cultured, shapely and personable – wearing a sleek black dress with a red pattern of streaks suggesting the long, thin leaves of some sort of vine.

It's not often I can remember my dreams and even the ones I think I have hold of when I wake up invariably drift off, beyond recall, within a few minutes. In this case, as vivid as it was, I doubt I would have remembered the name 'Fanvula' had I not written it down straight away.

Doing that is a habit developed by most writers who have some of their best ideas in the middle of the night, usually somewhere in the 'twilight zone'. There can be a phrase or a line of poetry. You don't want to wake yourself up properly so you lie in the dark and repeat it several times until you are certain it will be there, waiting, when you wake in the morning. It's good and you've perfected it – there's no doubt you'll remember it in the morning.

But inevitably when morning comes, not only is the line not there, but you have no idea what it was even about, much less remembering it in perfect detail.

But Jill did not escape. She was not a 'middle-of-the-night' visitor but one who was there the instant before I awoke for the day. I pounced on her name and wrote it down, well aware

I wasn't going to remember a name like 'Fanvula' if I didn't. And having captured her name, it seems I captured her, too.

I can still see her – medium height, slightly longer than medium-length dark hair with a hint of a wave, the black and red sheath dress and black patent leather high heels – not too high but high enough to be attractive and show off her legs without looking ridiculous.

It was night-time and we were in a crowded room at what must have been some sort of party. I don't know who else was there but I had the feeling I didn't know anyone and that she didn't either.

Analysing dreams is, at best, an imperfect science but I think I've managed to work out the reason for the black and red dress. The previous evening I had watched a football game on TV and the winners, Essendon, wear black and red. More than half of my closest friends barrack for Essendon so, despite the fact that I don't, the team's fortunes still occupy a prominent place in my mind.

So I'll assume that accounts for the dress, but where the rest of it came from, heaven knows.

I don't think I actually spoke to Jill, just admired her from afar, but there was no doubt about her name – I just don't know how I knew it.

I suspect that if it wasn't just a dream, I'd be wildly attracted to Jill Fanvula, so what do I do now? Maybe eat more 'dream-food', or watch more Essendon football matches, or just hope she knocks on my door?

But I'm properly awake now, so I realise that's probably not going to happen. I guess I'll just have to settle for having had a lovely dream, and being able to remember it.

As for Jill, it was nice to have nearly met her.

Nevertheless, I think I'll go and have a look at the electoral rolls, starting with 'F'.

The Rubbish Bin

He'd promised himself he wasn't going to be like them.

He'd been quite outspoken in his opinion that, despite their success, it was obvious they didn't own rubbish bins.

'Most people,' he'd said, 'know when they've written a piece of crap and they chuck it, but some of them don't waste anything – they just put it in a book.'

Their best stuff was great, he'd said, but their books were full of padding.

It didn't matter whether they were collections of short stories or poetry, there was a lot of it which should never have seen the light of day. He'd likened it to some of the albums he'd bought by popular recording artists – if you wanted the one good song, you had to put up with twenty others no-one had ever heard of.

He was determined not to do that but by his own admission he lacked imagination, which narrowed his available range of topics. It was common knowledge that most of his stories were based largely on personal experience, so there were times he had to be prudent in the way he wrote them.

For instance, he could hardly write about the murder. Revealing the intricate details would provide a great story but he'd been very careful and the whole investigation had quickly faded from prominence. The cops hadn't even found the knife and they wouldn't, he knew that.

Nevertheless, his writing career had flourished, his books were popular and he couldn't take the chance that one of the investigators was a fan who liked to read his short stories. It was probably unlikely but it was well-known that many of his stories were non-fiction so it wouldn't be smart to give them any sort of a lead by writing about it.

He knew that, of all the people in the office, he'd be considered to be the least likely to be what they called a 'person of interest'. He lived alone, kept to himself, didn't socialise and was on holiday the day it happened.

The cops had interviewed everyone, himself included, but all they'd really established was that the victim had the reputation of always being first to arrive at work and that he wasn't well liked.

His routine was well-known. He was always on the first train and walked from the station to the office, even during the winter when it was dark. Everyone knew that, so it didn't provide a clue and his lack of popularity and the number of people he'd offended hadn't done much to narrow down the list of possible suspects.

But the whole thing had pretty much gone away. The funeral hadn't been well-attended and the media had quickly moved on to their next expose.

So the bottom line was that none of it really helped. As much as he needed another good story to bolster his upcoming collection and as much as the murder would have provided great material, he was going to have to consign the idea, unwritten, to the rubbish bin.

He'd have to find something else. There are some things better left unwritten, for all sorts of reasons.

Catherine In Wonderland

SHE lay on her back, knees bent, legs spread, the child-woman with bruises in the creases of her elbows and along her forearms.

Eyes closed, with her mind in Wonderland, looking for Alice.

Above her he heaved and panted and grunted, thrusting against her pelvis.

He had told her his name, as if to make it more personal, but she hadn't been listening, or couldn't remember. He was fifty bucks.

She needed the money for the drugs. She needed the job for the money and she needed the drugs to be able to get through the job.

Perhaps he'd said his name was Barry, but what did it matter? Just another faceless face. Just another prick, in both senses of the word. 'Ha, I made a funny!' she thought.

The grunting had stopped and he lay on her. Heavy. Heavy enough to make her move, to half-wriggle out from underneath. He flopped sideways and lay motionless beside her, one arm draped across her. She fought the urge to sleep.

She knew the rules. Who cared if you were 'out of it', or just plain exhausted, sleep was not an option. It had happened once and had nearly cost her her job.

"F'Chrissakes Cathy," Belle had screamed at her, "what do you think you're doing..? You're not here to *sleep* with 'em..."

They'd sent her home in a cab and docked her pay, then she'd had to put up with one of Belle's lectures. Belle wasn't too bad really and what she'd said made a lot of sense.

"Cathy honey, they're not going to ask for you next time if you go to sleep in the middle of it. Half of 'em still think they're Rudolph bloody Valentino y'know."

That was all, but she knew that next time there wouldn't be a next time. There were plenty more junkies to take her place, or smug college girls 'working' their way through university.

"I'd rather have you, love," Belle had confided to her once. "Those other bitches think their shit doesn't stink…" What Belle really meant, though, was that the junkies were easier to control.

At least this was better than it used to be, she thought. The water-bed was comfortable, the room was immaculate but most of all it was safe. Or at least as close as you were going to get to safe. Not like the old days, months ago, stepping off the kerb into a car beside someone who wasn't going to change your life, but might end it.

The money wasn't as good now she had to give half of it away and it took twice as long, twice as many faceless freaks, to get enough. And how much was ever going to be enough? She had gone from pot through the whole list, downhill or uphill, depending on which way you thought of it – speed, crack, coke, ecstasy, then 'the real stuff', *horse*, the big H.

It cost her a fortune to support her habit but it was more reliable these days, more ordered. The cycle just kept going round – the 'faceless faces', the money, the drugs…

***

It had started four years ago, in another lifetime, when she was 12.

In those days she'd been Catherine, or at least she was to her grandpa, whom she adored. She remembered when she was a little girl, Grandpa sitting on the side of her bed reading her 'Alice In Wonderland'

"Where's Wonderland?" she'd asked him and Grandpa had told her it was just over the hill behind the big, white houses on Maple Road with their high fences and heavy, black wrought-iron gates and their shiny cars where they used to pass on the tram.

"Where does Alice live?" she'd ask him, standing on the seat as they went by, and occasionally Catherine would catch a glimpse of one of the elegantly-dressed ladies who lived in the houses and dream of the day she'd join them.

Catherine loved going with Grandpa past Wonderland and thought what good fun it would be to go with Alice to a tea-party.

Her mother had come home from the funeral drunk and abusive and there had been no more bedtime stories.

The other kids were smoking joints in the toilets or down in the far corner of the school ground, under the cypress trees where it was dry and the darkness of the shade provided a safe place to abandon safety.

Joining in hadn't seemed like any big deal at the time, it was just what everybody did. And anyway, the smoke made her feel good, grown-up, and it was easier to face going home to her drunken mother, who would belt the crap out of her, just for something to do.

Sometimes she'd get lucky and her mother would be passed out on the couch, or in the bedroom giggling and moaning with one of her pig boyfriends. Catherine hated them and the way they undressed her with their leering eyes and groped her when her mother wasn't looking.

The smoke made her feel euphoric and full of the joy of life. She'd mother her little sisters and bring in the washing if her mother had done it, or do it herself if she hadn't.

It was her thirteenth birthday, the day he had grabbed her and dragged her into the bedroom. She couldn't remember *his* name either, but she remembered his hideous, twitching prick and how he'd snatched a handful of her hair at the back of her head and pushed her face down onto it.

She remembered her clenched teeth, the pain as her head was jerked back and the whack of his butcher's hand across the side of her face.

"Open yer mouth ya little bitch…" he yelled and she had been too scared not to.

He shuddered and spurted and filled her mouth and her throat and released his grip and she retched and ran from the room and threw up on the lounge-room floor before she made it to the door.

She'd glimpsed her mother lying naked on the bed and assumed she was unconscious but hadn't been quite sure. She was sure the next time, though, because the next time her mother had been sitting up.

From then on it was always going to be easy for the sleaze in the schoolyard to sell the little white pills to Catherine, and easier for her to want them than to get the money to pay.

She wasn't stupid -- she knew how the other girls got money and at first it had been almost an adventure. She'd had money to spare and any was a lot when you'd been used to having none, but it was never going to last.

"Where did you get all this you little whore?" screamed her mother, bursting into the kitchen brandishing a fistful of notes as Catherine dropped her school-bag on the table.

"Don't *you* call *me* a whore," yelled Catherine, "and give me that…"

She surprised herself. She'd never stood up to her mother before, even when the old bitch had ransacked the place looking for grog money and emptied the little kids' money-boxes.

But it made no difference – Catherine didn't see the money again but noticed the next day there were half a dozen bottles of cheap Scotch in the corner instead of the usual one or two. That night she packed her worldly goods in a bag and met Deb on the corner as usual.

"Hi Cathy," came the greeting, "what's with the bag – ya runnin' away from home?"

"Yep," she'd replied, "I'm comin' to live with you."

Living with Deb was fine. They laughed a lot and she didn't miss school one bit. They'd sleep half the day and work half the night and spend most of the time spaced out on the stuff Deb got for both of them from the lunk she liked to refer to as her 'manager'. She missed her sisters and she missed her grandpa and she missed Wonderland, but mostly life was just a haze with soft edges and it didn't really seem to matter any more.

But Catherine knew that it *did* matter. Sure, she was Cathy now, but the Catherine her grandpa had loved still lived somewhere down inside and just occasionally, when the tram took her along Maple Road, it would all come back.

One day, she would live in one of the big white houses, she mused.

***

Somewhere in the background Billy Joel sang 'Piano Man'.

"...I'm sure that I could be a movie star,
*   if I could get out of this place..."*

It all seemed so long ago, she thought.

Barry had lumbered to his feet and started putting on his clothes.

The Race

"ON YOUR MARKS..!" commanded the starter.

A hush fell over the stadium.

It had come to this. This moment. The focus of my life. The hours, the sweat, the toil, the money, the sacrifices. It had come to this.

It had started in the schoolyard at Murchison the day I raced Jimmy Tweddle.

Mr. Milvain, the teacher, was casting the school play. It was about the Trojan War and how Pheidippides had run from the Battle of Marathon to Sparta with news of victory over the invading Persian army. It was important that the best runner in the school play the part of Pheidippides and no-one was sure whether that was Jimmy Tweddle or me. Except me, of course. I was sure.

Not that whoever played Pheidippides was going to have to do any more than jog across the stage carrying what was supposed to be the Olympic torch. He certainly wasn't going to have to sprint the length of the schoolyard and crash into the old wooden fence like I had to do to be sure no-one could say I hadn't beaten Jimmy Tweddle fair and square. And he certainly wasn't going to have to run the 140 miles Pheidippides did, nor even the classic marathon distance of 26 miles and 385 yards so many glory-driven Olympic athletes have done since. But it had to be done properly, nevertheless.

I ran a marathon once. I guess for me that was the beginning of the *real* running, but before the *serious* stuff started. Before I was told I had 'potential' and that I should be doing other things.

I don't remember the whole of the marathon, but bits of it seem like yesterday. Like catching the train at 3.30am to take us to the start (because it was a one-way course, as opposed to 'out-and-back'). The carriage-full of bleary-eyed, weirdly-dressed, diverse specimens of humanity, smelling of liniment, smeared with Vaseline and mostly looking like they'd just been evicted from their St.Vincent de Paul clothing collection bins.

I remember standing in the middle of 8000 like-minded idiots, wearing a large plastic garbage bag upside-down over my running gear, head and arms sticking out of the pre-cut holes, waiting in the cold for the 7am start.

Then the race. Turning into Beach Road and the headwind hitting us in the face. God, was it going to be like this for the last 34 kilometres? This bloke running with the group of about 10 of us, dashing into a beach-front milk bar, catching up again a couple of minutes later and passing around jelly-beans. Then later someone else disappearing into another shop and coming out with a bag of icy poles. Sweaty runners taking a bite and handing them on to whoever was running beside them.

Then the pain, the jolting, searing, all-over aching pain and 'the wall' that marathon runners talk about, which you think is a load of bull until *you* hit it.

I remember the endless road, stretching as far ahead as you're brave enough to look. You fix your eyes on a building far, far in the distance and every time you look up to check, it doesn't seem to be any closer, until suddenly you look and it's gone, it's behind you.

And there's the 'rush' (they say it's the release of the body's endorphins), 'the runner's high'. The mind senses the finishing line and the body lifts and the legs begin to stride at a rate which, at that stage, should be impossible. The exhilaration. There's not another feeling like it in the world.

A marathon is not about running a race, or about finishing positions, or even time. It is about aloneness within a herd and single-minded determination to do something that makes no sense. It is about being in one distinct group of people on the planet as opposed to the other group. Being one of those who *have* gone the distance, and understand what it's about, as opposed to those who *haven't*, and to whom it cannot possibly be explained.

Running a marathon is about experiencing something unique in life!

That was a long time ago. Firmly in the past, in the 'OUT' basket – done. These days I run only one lap of the track, seldom less, never more. The firm, rubberised, leg-friendly, brick-coloured road to nowhere, each lane precise between its two white lines, measured, exact.

The transition took ages, valuable years, transforming 'slow-twitch' fibres to 'fast-twitch'. From plod to power. The 'twitch' fibres in your muscles are what you're born with – 'fast' for speed, 'slow' for endurance --and undoubtedly mine were fast-twitch in the first place. No doubt, in retrospect, I should have stuck to sprinting. But my mind made my legs run a marathon and they lost their zing.

The whole process would have been a lot easier and more sensible without the marathon. A more natural progression. From sprinting across the school yard to sprinting around a track. Simple. Except for the mind part, the experience. Except for the memories and the pride. The *understanding*. The road I'd taken made no sense but I wouldn't have had it any other way.

The road back, from 'slow' to 'fast', was one of frustration. Torn muscles, pulled ligaments, aching legs. Perhaps a pure-bred sprinter might have given up. But a marathon runner – never!

The sessions and their variety were endless. Speed sessions, strength sessions, rhythm, technique, lactic sessions, gym, pool, recovery sessions, drills, repetitions, stretching, time trials, motivation, speed-endurance sessions.

And gradually it all returned. The speed, the purity of technique, the endurance under pressure. Gradually the body adapted – the legs learned about speed and power, the body about grace and poise, the mind about fine-tuning, the persona about care and nurturing, the brain about time, precision, rhythm. The athlete learned to run fast. The body learned to relax at high speed. To flow.

I already knew how to compete, to be competitive. Had I been any other way I would not have hit the school fence so hard the day I beat Jimmy Tweddle. I hadn't needed to, as it turned out, but I hadn't known that at the time. I couldn't take that risk. Not then, not now. Getting beaten didn't bear thinking about. It happened, of course, but if you'd done your best and knew it, you hadn't been beaten at all.

Courage, I'd always thought, went hand in hand with self-discipline. I wasn't sure that was how others saw it, but that was the way I saw it, which was all that mattered to me. I knew self-discipline could be learned but I wasn't so sure about courage. Maybe you had to be born with it. But nothing was ever won by courage alone. Success, in sport anyway, was more about iron will, guts and wanting something badly enough.

And I knew, as I settled on my blocks, that I wanted it badly enough.

I knew that Walter Bauer was in the lane next to me. Walter Bauer who had driven me, asleep in his bed in Germany, as I reeled off rep after rep, alone in the wind and scudding, icy rain, through the long winter months at the training track.

Walter Bauer, who had beaten me the only time we'd met in a race.

Only I knew the part Walter Bauer played in my training, and in my life.

"Where are you now, Walter Bauer?" the voice in my head would ask as I rounded the last bend and the wind and the sleet hit me straight in the face.

"You're at home in your bed and I'm training and you're not…I'm gaining on you Walter Bauer!" the voice would proclaim as I found myself gritting my teeth.

"Relax…relax..," the voice would tell me, "hold your stride, use your arms, run to the line."

It wasn't *all* Walter Bauer, but on those days when the wind and the rain bit into my flesh and every muscle and sinew screamed in pain, he was always there, a hundred metres from the line. He was *always* there.

And now it had come to this.

I took a deep breath and gently leaned forward, shoulders above my hands, fingers spread, bridged behind the freshly-painted white line glistening against the brick-red track.

Briefly, my gaze followed the curving line of my lane to where the first flight of hurdles gleamed black-and-white in the summer sun.

Slowly, I lowered my eyes and dropped my head.

I waited…

"SET..!"

Apart from some minor 'poetic licence', this story is true. Trembath and Bauer met only once more, in the final of the World Masters' Championship 300 metres hurdles in Riccione, Italy, in 2007. In a three-way photo-finish for second place, Bauer ran third with Trembath fourth

The Faces of Love

The Abandoned Golliwog

Golly couldn't understand it. How had it come to this? – lying beside a charity bin, with nary a friend in sight.

It had been bad enough being in the wardrobe for all those years, but at least it hadn't been solitary confinement, there had been quite a few of his friends from when he was young.

Then the joy of release and having the world around him once again. But the world seemed different and where was his little girl?

Golly remembered long, long ago, how excited she'd been when they met – her very first golliwog. She'd cuddled him and taken him to bed and he'd been to tea parties with all his friends and she'd shown him off to all the other little girls who'd come to their house to play.

But Golly didn't realise that he'd been born (or knitted actually) in another era, before PC had overtaken the world. Over the years he'd listened to conversations through the wardrobe door and he'd often heard PC mentioned but had always imagined they were referring to PC Plod – Mr Plod the Policeman -- and he knew all about him from the stories his little girl's Mummy would read them at bedtime.

It seemed a little strange to Golly, though, that PC was the only one from those days that anyone talked about any more. He remembered his little girl's Mummy teaching her nursery rhymes like 'Baa baa black sheep, have you any wool?' but he hadn't heard about 'Baa baa black sheep' in ages and how could PC Plod have taken over the world?

It was all most puzzling and Golly lay there, wondering what was going to happen next.

He'd wondered various things over the past few years in fact, in particular why no-one had bothered to sew his eye back on when the thread broke and the little buttons fell off. Still, he had one good eye and he supposed he should be grateful – after all, some of his fellow wardrobe dwellers were missing all sorts of things, arms, legs and one poor dolly didn't even have a head.

There had been people walking past all day and not one of them had given him a second glance until suddenly a nice man and a nice lady had stopped and said: 'Look at that poor abandoned golliwog.'

'If he's still there when we come back, he can come home with me,' said the nice man.

'You're mad,' said the nice lady, and off they went.

A long time passed – not years, like wardrobe time, but hours, which seem like a long time when you're lying lonely beside a charity bin.

Then, just as despair was setting in again, back came Nice Man and Nice Lady.

They stopped, and Golly listened to the conversation.

'No wonder he's here,' said Nice Man, 'he fulfils all the criteria for finishing up on Society's scrap heap.'

'Well he sure won't have any of the PC mob rescuing him,' said Nice Lady. 'Everyone knows golliwogs aren't politically correct these days and look at him, he's black, he's disabled – look at his eye – he's homeless and he's unloved.'

Golly was shocked. He knew he was black and he knew one eye was missing, but 'homeless and unloved…?' What about his little girl? Where was she and why hadn't she come to rescue him?

'It's sad,' said Nice Lady. 'Somebody loved him once.'

'Loved him once? ' thought Golly. 'Does that mean she doesn't love me now?' And suddenly, through his one button-eye, Golly saw the light.

His little girl had grown up, which was probably why he hadn't seen her in years, and Mr Plod the Policeman wasn't going to come and take him home.

'What's going to become of me?,' thought Golly, then suddenly his question was answered.

'He's coming home with me,' said Nice Man to Nice Lady as he bent down and took him by the hand, brushing the leaves off his back.

'What are you going to do with him?' asked Nice Lady.

'I'll offer him to my friend Valerie, to be a playmate for her new pussycat and if she doesn't want him, he can come home with me and he can hang out with Sherlock (who just happens to be a cardboard cut-out dog).

'I reckon he'll get along with Valerie's cat. Her name is Dammi, which is short for 'Damsel In Distress', because she was in a predicament very similar to Golly's.'

'The only trick might be that Dammi's snow-white and Golly's black, but I don't think cats and golliwogs have any problem with racial prejudice, do they?'

Golly didn't know what 'racial prejudice' was and he certainly didn't have any, so home he went with Nice Man, then next morning he met Valerie.

'Oh, isn't he lovely,' she exclaimed, 'Dammi will love him.'

Valerie showed him to her girlfriends and as he listened to their conversation he gradually realised he was going somewhere where there was no PC, no wardrobe and that love was coming back into his life.

He wasn't exactly sure what they'd said or what it meant but it sounded exciting and he couldn't help being swept up in a wave of joy and anticipation as he set off with Valerie for the next chapter in his new adventure.

'I'm going for a ride in a big washing machine,' he smiled to himself.

He didn't know what that meant either, but it sounded exciting.

Throwing Out the Love

You want a difficult job? Try cleaning up sometime.

Not the house, or the garage, or the tool-shed. Try sorting through the greeting cards you've accumulated over the years.

The birthday cards, the 'get well' cards, the Christmas cards and all the others that define the life you've led.

You know if you don't throw them out, someone else will, when you're gone. Make the job easier for them. Throw out the love.

Throw out the love? How do you do that?

You start your task. The ghosts of friends long gone glide from the pages of their cards and transform into memories.

You pause, think fondly of them, and then consign the card to the ever-growing pile that has to go. You remind yourself you're saving someone else the trouble.

The pile grows, as does the congregation of friends in your head. People who have passed through your life briefly. Those who have stayed longer. A few who are still there. People you haven't thought of for years. Where are they now? What happened? How did you drift apart?

Perhaps you wanted to drift, or they did – it only takes one. You look upon the evidence that once they were there, and consign the card to the pile. The memory has been 'noted' but that's all.

There is another list, of course, of the myriad people you've been meaning to 'catch up with', some of them for years, but never have. You used to know their birthdays. Perhaps they still know yours. Is there a message there?

The birthday cards are the hardest. Christmas cards are nice to receive, but there's a part of them which is about

Christmas and not just about you. Birthday cards are different. They recognise your special day – they're about caring, and love. *They're* about you.

But you overcome the pain, you cherish the memories, and they go on the pile.

But then there are the ones for birthdays which end in a 'zero' – milestones in your life. They're special. You procrastinate – and start a second pile. It will only be a small pile and it won't present a problem later, but they're reminders of the memories. They have to stay.

And then there's one which starts 'My Darling' and ends with 'All my love'. It's from a shining time, not really long ago, but gone. It only serves to enhance the memory. You pause, reflect – and put it on the second pile. It's not the only one, of course, but they're not going anywhere.

The cards create a memory lane, a passing parade of friends and lovers, of good times in your life. But they're not important to anyone but you and you know, you've told yourself, that you're doing someone a favour in leaving a very small pile instead of a very big one.

So you grit your teeth and do it.

But you can't help but think you're throwing out the love.

The Most Beautiful Girl in the World

Today, sitting in the spring sunshine watching the passing parade in the city square in Athens, I saw the most beautiful girl in the world.

She was statuesque, wearing a black top with faded jeans she must have been born in, which flared, as if an afterthought, above stiletto-heeled, jewelled sandals.

The light breeze played with her long, raven hair as she strolled across the square. I would have followed her anywhere. In fact, thirty years ago I may well have done.

She stopped and half-turned, rummaged in her bag, and threw something to a pigeon.

Then, like a soft breeze, she continued to the far edge of the square.

She paused, glanced sideways, and, as the traffic lights changed, merged into the crowd.

I watched until she was a part of it, then took another sip of my coffee.

The Plan

'So what are you two giggling about?' he asked.

It was quite unusual to hear giggling in the hospital, especially in the palliative care ward.

But here they were, carrying on like a couple of teenagers, which hadn't been the case for quite a few decades.

He'd been away for nearly half an hour. He was going to the café for a coffee, he'd told them, but he'd spent most of the time wandering around the grounds, unusually appreciative of the gardens, aware of the beauty of the flowers he'd driven past so many times in the previous couple of months without really noticing.

His absence had very little to do with coffee although he brought three takeaway cups back to Kim's room, where she was sitting propped up on her pillows, with Valerie leaning in as they plotted and giggled.

No-one had mentioned it was the last time they'd see each other but he knew and was very aware that they knew – it was what is sometimes described as the elephant in the room.

Kim had been in hospital, on and off, for about six months now, more regularly in recent times since the operation. The cancer had become more aggressive and they'd hoped the last operation might have got all of it, but it hadn't happened. Now it was only a matter of time.

He'd introduced Kim to Valerie several years earlier and they'd gradually formed a close friendship, so much so that Kim's final text message to her friend had been that she wished she could adopt her as a sister.

Valerie had seen Kim fight off the first bout of cancer and had marvelled at the resilience she'd shown in coming back from death's door to normal good health. The three of them all knew about the blood tests but after a while they had become routine. They knew the figures weren't perfect, but they were good enough that when she went for her periodic appointments, the oncologist was smiling and upbeat.

Kim had worked hard to get fit with regular running, exercise classes and gym work and it had come as a surprise the day the doctor told her that her blood readings had taken a significant turn for the worse. It was back to the chemotherapy and radiation she'd been through four years earlier, but the determination remained – she was going to beat this. And at one stage it seemed she was going to be right.

They went to her next appointment not expecting much, only to have the oncologist tell her that 90 per cent of the cancer was gone. They left the waiting room high-fiving and got on with life.

But sometimes, when something seems too good to be true, it's because it isn't. She had another round of blood tests and was feeling good. They went to the next appointment confident the doctor was going to give her the all clear but what he said was that the 90 per cent had regressed to 80 per cent. Looking back later, that was the turning point.

And here she was, lying back against the pillows, talking to Valerie for the last time.

Kim had been talking for a while now about wanting to end it all – to put an end to the pain and to what her body had become. He'd asked her at one stage whether, if she had a pill on her bedside table, she would take it or not.

'Some days I would, some days I wouldn't,' she'd replied. Hardly the answer the pro-euthanasia lobby would want to hear. But there were no doubts when told someone was praying for her. She hoped they were praying for the right thing – that it was going to be over as soon as possible.

There was no way, of course, that Kim was going to be able to influence her own destiny, despite the plan she and Valerie had come up with during the time he was away getting the coffee.

Valerie was well aware her own issues were not in the same league as Kim's, but she'd had a problem for months now and was looking forward to the hip replacement operation which was scheduled for the following week. She was in constant pain and frustrated that her usual fit, active lifestyle had been compromised. She'd told Kim she was sick of herself and sometimes felt like jumping off a bridge.

The two related to each other's problems, without addressing them too closely – their friendship was too valuable for that. They revelled in each other's company and were determined to make the most of it while they could.

The giggling subsided as he handed the coffees around. But he still wanted to know what had led to such levity in these most unlikely surroundings.

'We've got a plan,' they told him, grinning together like a couple of naughty schoolgirls.

'We're going to ring a taxi and get him to take us down to sit on the railway tracks.'

And they both managed to look like the cat that had swallowed the cream.

Stealing the Love

There had been times when he'd thought he was over her, back to normal (whatever that was), but they had turned out to be illusions, transitory, brief moments of respite.

There had been times he'd thought he should take her photo down, or at least not look at it every time he entered the room.

'Move on,' his friends had told him, 'you've grieved enough.' But what was going to be 'enough'?

He had known he was going to lose her, that he was going to have to live the rest of his life without her, but he hadn't expected it to be like this. Not like this, keen-edged – not after this long.

He thinks he loves her even more now, which seems impossible, but perhaps that's because it's so much easier to remember the good bits – in fact he struggles now to recall any bad bits, although he knows there were some.

Sometimes he wonders if he'll ever let her go. It's been six years now, but sometimes it seems like maybe two, or twenty-two.

Their two closest friends still go with him, each year, to the special place she loved, to celebrate her birthday and her life.

The kookaburras which swoop to steal their lunch weren't born when she was there. The rough-hewn wooden table was, and the trees and the river. Nothing has changed, or nearly nothing, except that she's not there.

Her spirit is everywhere, all around, surrounding their picnic site, along the river track and floating in the gentle breeze. In the bush, around each bend, across the wooden bridges and up and down each undulation.

He recalls the days they ran the journey to the far end of the track, when they'd pull up panting and laughing, revelling in each other's exhaustion, then turn around and do it all again.

These days the three of them – three of the four – still do that on her birthday, then come back to the table, drink a champagne toast and have their picnic. And the kookaburras still swoop. They can steal the lunch, but not the memories.

And even time can't steal the love.

Copyright / Acknowledgments

Without You and *But Once* were first performed on Radio 3UZ, Melbourne.

When Did The Roses Die and *Corporate Irrelevance* were first performed on Radio 3AW, Melbourne.

The Tree On Gibbet Hill was first published in The Australian Way, Qantas Airways.

Life's Path, While Love Remains, Morning Dew, On Parting and *And Time Will Pass* were previously published in *More Lives Than One*.

Rest Easy, Girl, The Race and *Catherine In Wonderland* were previously published in *In The Company Of Strangers*. The latter two both won prizes in the 2005 edition of the Alan Marshall Short Story Awards.

About the Author

Richard Trembath has led a life of many facets and has generally been regarded by those who know him as a most unlikely poet.

Orphaned at 16 after growing up in the tiny town of Walwa, in the Upper Murray Valley, he spent most of his working life as a journalist specialising in horse racing, first with one of Melbourne's major newspaper companies, the Herald Sun, then with its main competitor, The Age.

He combined this with his passion for the 'hands on' aspect of harness racing, breeding, training and driving horses in races for 35 years, during which time he won several of the sport's major events as well as numerous journalistic awards for literary excellence, photography and video documentaries. He also had four of his songs released commercially.

Trembath was an inaugural member of harness racing's Hall of Fame but in later years returned to his boyhood love of athletics, winning ten Australian Masters' Athletics Championships, at one stage being ranked No 1 in the world in his age-group in long hurdles. He was also heavily involved in the administration of the sport and managed one of Masters' Athletics' most successful venues for many years.

During all this time, however, he continued to write poetry and short stories, If We Should Ever Meet Again being his third book. He prides himself in writing poetry which 'the man in the street' understands and appreciates.

Like his two previous books, If We Should Ever Meet Again presents a cross-section of Trembath's poetry, short stories and award-winning newspaper and magazine stories.

Trembath is divorced, with four adult children, and lives in an outer suburb of Melbourne.